About the Author

Maria Valentine was born in London's East End and has worked in education for many years. Never wanting to be too far from the sea, she has spent time living in various coastal locations, before finally settling in Southwold, Suffolk. Here she likes to spend her time at the beach, walking, reading, and writing her stories whilst listening to the sounds of the sea. *The Weekend Game* is Maria's first novella. She is currently writing her first novel, *Making it Happen*, and is also compiling a series of short stories.

The Weekend Game

Maria Valentine

The Weekend Game

Olympia Publishers
London

www.olympiapublishers.com
OLYMPIA PAPERBACK EDITION

A CIP catalogue record for this title is
available from the British Library.

ISBN: 978-1-80439-425-0

This is a work of fiction.
Names, characters, places and incidents originate from the writer's
imagination. Any resemblance to actual persons, living or dead, is
purely coincidental.

First Published in 2023

Olympia Publishers
Tallis House
2 Tallis Street
London
EC4Y 0AB

Printed in Great Britain

Acknowledgements

With thanks to Val, for being my writing buddy, my proofreader, my sounding board, my friend. It's your turn now...

Chapter 1

Let me tell you about Toula and James.

James Miller is in his early thirties. He has lived by the beach his whole life and has mostly taken it for granted. He plays cricket for the local team every Saturday afternoon and goes out for drinks in the evening with the same group of boys he grew up with. He loves his family and sees his mum for dinner every Thursday. He went to university to study sports science and coaching when his chance to play professional cricket fell through because of an injury. He dropped out and came home when his father fell ill. He has worked at the station for the last six years and has no idea how he got through Toula's interview without turning into a dribbling wreck, so captivated was he from the first moment he saw her sitting in the lobby.

Toula George is three years older than James, although you'd never know it. She was lucky enough to inherit her grandmother's genes and still, on occasion, gets asked for ID in bars which she finds incredibly flattering, sometimes to the point of smugness. She has always lived in the city but moved to the coast for a complete life overhaul following the devastating heartbreak caused by the end of what she thought was the perfect relationship with the person she would be spending the rest of her life with. She has just moved into a one-bedroom cottage which overlooks the dunes at the far end of the beach. The only person she knows here is the guy who makes her hot chocolates in the pier café at the other end of the beach, whom she met one weekend while she was house hunting. She has four job interviews lined up this week and had better get one of them because, perhaps against her better judgment, she's bought the house already, and her savings won't pay the mortgage forever.

James interviewed three other women that day, knowing, with one hundred per cent clarity, that he wouldn't be hiring any of them. As he had seen the last one out, James told himself that he would wait until the morning to call Toula; he didn't want to seem too eager but was unable to stop himself from picking up the phone as soon as he had got back to the office.

Following her interview, Toula headed straight to the café on the pier where she sat in a large leather armchair by the picture window overlooking the bay, reading her book, and drinking hot chocolate. The view was incredible, with the sun setting over the sea and the sky quickly turning to the deepest shade of blue with a shot of gold separating it from the ocean, and she soon found herself transfixed, the book forgotten in her lap. When her phone rang, it made her jump.
"Hello," she said.

James even liked the way Toula answered the phone. He really needed to pull himself together. *Get a grip, Miller.* As professionally as he could manage, James thanked Toula for her time that day and offered her the job. He wanted her to start as soon as possible, so her response knocked the wind out of his sails. He hadn't anticipated anything other than her accepting, yet here she was, asking if she could let him know on Friday as she had three other interviews lined up.

"Friday?" James heard himself scream internally. Friday was three days away. Ever the professional, though, out loud he said,

"Of course, that's absolutely fine. Have a great week, and we'll catch up on Friday. Good luck with your other interviews," he said, not really meaning it.

The next three days flew by for Toula; she skipped through her remaining interviews confidently, secure in the knowledge that she had James's offer already in the bag.

By Thursday, she had added another two offers to that one. She was not qualified for the last job but had taken a punt purely because she thought the building was beautiful, so she was not surprised or disappointed to hear that she had been unsuccessful.

That evening, feeling brave, she headed into town to treat herself to dinner at that place on the corner she had felt was far too cool for her to be at, but she decided that she didn't care. She ordered a peach mojito and mussels with thick, crusty bread and a side of fries. Toula ate at the bar where she got chatting with the barman and, over the course of the evening, hashed out all the pros and cons of each job. By the time Toula left, she had made a decision and a new friend.

James's week dragged on as he waited impatiently for Toula's decision. He found that he was unable to concentrate at work or home. He was restless and couldn't settle on anything. He was completely unfocused during his Wednesday night cricket training and hardly said two words to his mum during dinner on Thursday. In short, he was a

11

mess. He couldn't understand it, he had never been like this over a woman before and was very much aware that, even when he wasn't consciously thinking about her, she was always there, somewhere, in the back of his mind.

People around him were noticing this change in him. He fobbed them off, saying he was tired, not sleeping, it was an injury playing up, stuff going on at work; whatever popped into his head.

By Friday morning, he had given up trying to get anything done that took any actual thought and instead rearranged his office. He had just finished putting everything back where it had been initially when the phone rang.

James forced himself to take three deep breaths and then answered the phone. Toula accepted the job. She'd see him a week on Monday. He slumped back down in his chair. Now he was in trouble.

Toula and James hit it off immediately. They talked constantly and found they had much in common, not just the superficial stuff like food, music, movies, and ideal holiday destinations, but life goals and dreams, values, and beliefs. By the end of the first week of working together, he had told her how he felt about her.

Now they were both in trouble.

Let's skip forward ten months and see what these two are up to now…

Chapter 2

It was Friday morning, the sun was not quite up yet. Mornings had been darker for longer lately, but the skies had been clear and so the sun used this to her advantage, treating everyone to stunning displays of colour. Today, she had chosen that beautiful shade of pink you find on the inside of a conch shell. As if competing for the title of *Most Beautiful Act of Nature,* the sea sparkled silver, like a ribbon stretching across the horizon, embellished with sequins and jewels.

"Would you look at that?"

"We are so lucky to have this on our doorstep."

"Perfect view."

Sadly, today was a workday so there was no time to enjoy it. Toula would have loved to go for a walk along the beach this morning, and, as she turned the car into the next road, leaving the view behind them, James squeezed her leg gently. He felt the same.

Toula sighed, content.

Friday mornings usually meant breakfast rolls and coffees from the drive-thru on the roundabout, but they needed to take milk in to work, so they headed to the convenience store down the street instead. They should have left earlier so they could have done both, or even been more organised yesterday.

James jumped out of the car.

"Do you want anything?" he asked, already knowing the answer; she was one of those annoying people who said, "Surprise me."

He usually just bought them both a pain au chocolate, and they would drop crumbs everywhere while they ate during their journey. By the time they got out, the car would look like someone had been throwing confetti around. They took turns hoovering the car each weekend. Today was different; he got back in the car and handed Toula a bar of chocolate.

"*Marvellous Creation*? What's one of those?"

"I have no idea, but I got it because you are a marvellous creation too."

Toula laughed, rolling her eyes. He was so cute but SO cheesy!

Work passed in an uneventful blur, the highlight of the day being when they found themselves unexpectedly alone in the office.

Toula sat at her desk, eating her chocolate. She could feel him watching her as she ate but didn't look up. Suddenly an explosion in her mouth made her giggle.

"What's going on over there?"

"There's popping candy in my *Marvellous Creation*."

Mischief lit up his eyes, and in one easy movement, James was out of his chair and walking towards her.

"Then there's now popping candy in my marvellous creation." He broke off a piece of the chocolate, put it in his mouth, and then pulled Toula towards him. Their kiss was a chocolatey, popping, fizzing delight. Their own marvellous creation indeed!

On the journey home, they played *The Weekend Game*.

They played it every Friday, and it involved nothing more than planning their perfect weekend. This week was James' turn.

He pulled into the parking space at Waitrose, making sure that the car was facing the sunset over the hill, put Toula's favourite playlist on, and kissed her quickly before jumping out of the car. Ten minutes later, he was back with bags full of goodies, refusing to answer her questions about what was in them.

Back at home, James dumped the bags on the kitchen counter and ran upstairs, calling,

"Don't unpack them!" as he went.

She could hear the bath water running and the click-click of a lighter, followed by soft music. This guy was too good to be true.

She followed him upstairs and found him putting her book and a fresh fluffy towel on the chair next to the bath. He twirled her around and kissed her hand.

"You relax; dinner will be in an hour."

The evening continued as wonderfully as it had begun.

Garlic prawn linguine preceded mango sorbet and cocktails. They took their drinks through to the lounge, where James had lit the fire and more candles. Toula sank into the cosy cushions on the sofa while James fiddled with the TV remote. He sat down, and she snuggled into him as *Jaws* burst onto the screen. Toula couldn't help but laugh. He was getting lots of points for this evening.

Toula woke before James the following morning, feeling happy. She couldn't stop smiling. She threw on the shirt he had worn yesterday which had been flung on the chair when they had come to bed last night, and went down to the kitchen.

She tossed coffee into the cafetiere and croissants into the oven. James was still sleeping, a slight smile playing on his lips when Toula took the loaded tray back upstairs. She put it down on the floor and climbed back into bed. As she did so, James woke up and pulled her towards him, wrapping her in his arms and kissing her with urgency. She moaned in pleasure.

It was lunchtime before they had eaten, showered, and bundled themselves up in all their winter clothes. James drove along the coast for around forty minutes, during which time they sang - well, Toula sang, James never did - chatted, and drank takeaway drinks from the drive-thru on the roundabout. It seemed like no time at all before they reached their destination; the forest.

James parked the car by the visitor centre. The afternoon was bright with sunlight streaming through the trees, the crisp air snatching their breath away. Toula watched him walk back from the payment machine and felt the smile on her face spread throughout her body. She loved how relaxed she felt with him like she could just be herself and didn't have to *try* constantly. It was a very freeing feeling.

James took her gloved hand in his, and they set off along the path.

The forest was busy, sunshine having lured people from their homes for a walk; families, couples, runners, dog walkers, all out in force on the main route, so Toula and James decided to get off the trail and make their own way. It was a little darker than on the path, the trees had not been thinned out here so the sun struggled to reach them through the heavy-set branches. It was muddier here, too, and a few times, Toula had to grab hold of James or a nearby branch to keep from falling over. She had always loved the forest and was enjoying exploring and climbing, slipping and sliding. They laughed a lot that afternoon, glad to have escaped the masses and have this part of the forest almost entirely to themselves. They saw two deer, some kind of weasley-stoaty thing, and a green woodpecker.

"Can you hear running water?" Toula asked as James lifted her down from a large rock she had climbed over and was now stuck on.

"I can. I didn't know there was a waterfall here. Let's go find it."

They followed the sound down the bank, clinging to tree branches and roots as they eased themselves down. Edging around a ledge, they could see the mist that was thrown back up as the fall hit the river below it. There it was.

Overhanging trees hid its top, which could have easily been forty feet up, and there was a cavern at the bottom on the other side of the river. The streaming sun kissed the spray, creating rainbows. It was incredible, so beautiful.

James turned Toula around so that the waterfall and rainbows were behind them and took a photo, kissing her on the cheek as he did so. He captured the moment perfectly. By the time they had climbed back up to the main trail, the sun had begun to set and, on reaching the car, they noticed the trees had turned to silhouettes against a background of flame.

Toula assumed they would be heading straight home so was pleasantly surprised when James pulled into the car park of a country pub that she had always liked the look of but, for one reason or another, had yet to visit.

Inside, it was cosy and warm, low ceilings with beams stripped back to their original state, and pale grey walls, deep comfy armchairs, and soft lighting. They grabbed a table by the huge, roaring fire, pulled their chairs around next to each other, and watched the flames dancing.

They ate fish tacos topped with the best coleslaw Toula had ever eaten. Huge chunky chips complemented their meal which they washed down with ginger beer. Toula laughed as the contents of her taco plopped out and onto her plate, leaving a trail of mayonnaise along her wrist, which James took in his hand, brought up to his lips, and licked clean.

They finished their meal and followed it up with coffee and card games. James loved how outrageously competitive Toula was, given that they were playing a game that she had only just taught him. Eventually, with the fire dying down and the pub emptying, he took her hand,

"Let's go home."

Sunday was a lazy day. They slept late and then went to the Greek deli on the High Street for brunch. It was bitterly cold out, and the clouds hung heavy as though filled with snow, despite none having been forecast.

Again, they lingered over their meal, this time talking about the many pictures on the walls. They both loved Greece and had seen it very differently. James through sailing holidays with his parents and sisters, learning to swim in the bottomless, crystal-clear Aegean Sea, catching fish and octopus which his dad had then barbecued on the back of the boat, falling in teenage love with a new girl on every island and not having the courage to talk to any of them. His last trip had been the year his dad passed away. They had gone sailing, just the two of them, drinking Metaxa, which his mother had never let him drink when he was younger, while his dad told stories about his own adventures growing up.

Toula had been to a few of the islands with girlfriends, weeks spent partying all night and exploring in the afternoons when they had finally managed to drag themselves out of bed. She had last visited following her break up last year. They had booked to go together and, after a month of crying and wallowing, she had woken up one morning and decided to go on her own. The holiday had been booked in her name and she had the tickets, all she needed was the courage to do it, which she found, somehow, and which the attention from the cute barman at the hotel intensified.

Now, they talked about their favourite places in Greece and where they would like to visit together. The rest of the afternoon was spent in front of the fire at home. James watched the cricket while Toula sat curled up in her rocking chair, reading.

"You're too far away," he said, putting down his coffee. He scooped her up in his arms and carried her over to the sofa. Toula laughed.

"You're so cute."

James kissed her deeply, and they both returned to what they had been doing, only now with her wrapped up in his arms.

Chapter 3

The following week sped by in a blur of meetings and end-of-year reports. They barely had two minutes to themselves at work or in the evenings, what with a yoga class, cricket training and family commitments. They'd had no time for coffees or breakfast muffins this morning but now it was Friday, clocking-off time, and they were heading home.

As Toula started the car, James handed her something. She turned it over to discover that it was a bar of *Wispa Gold* chocolate with the tagline, *Grab hold of the gold.*

"I saw it in the vending machine and thought of you." He winked, and Toula couldn't wait to hear his reasoning.

"Go on…" she said, as seriously as she could muster.

"Well, you're like gold dust, aren't you? And I can't wait to grab hold of you." James lunged towards her, kissing her neck while she let out a noise somewhere between a shriek and a laugh.

Pushing him off, Toula said, "Come on, let's get going, it's time for *The Weekend Game.*"

James sat back in his seat and put on his seatbelt, "I know it's technically your turn this week, but I have an idea."

"OK, fire away… What do you wanna do this weekend?"

"You," came his reply.

Toula smiled, her eyes twinkling mischievously, "Take

the wheel for a second."

James did as he was told; luckily, they were on a straight bit of road because his attention was somewhat distracted by the fact that Toula was wriggling out of her underwear, flashing the lacey tops of her stockings as she did so.

We're going to leave Friday evening there. And the whole of Saturday while we're at it, because I'm not that *kind of author and this is not* that *kind of book...*

On Sunday morning, James woke to the smell of coffee and bacon and the sound of Toula singing *Mack the Knife*, his favourite song. He quickly threw on a pair of joggers and a t-shirt and made his way downstairs, where he found Toula dancing around in a tiny pair of pyjama shorts and one of his hoodies.

James watched her for a while, a huge smile spreading across his face - Christ, she was adorable. He then put on what he thought was his stern voice, but which she always found hilarious, and said,

"Woman, you've half-killed me this weekend, now quit all this dancing; man needs his food!"

Toula spun around, laughing, and slapped James playfully with the spatula in her hand.

"Pour the coffee while I dish up, or I'll finish you off!"

Over breakfast, they did the crossword in the *Waitrose Weekend* magazine and tore out the pages of recipe ideas, which they would later stick into their recipe scrapbook. Toula had never really enjoyed cooking before she met James, but he was teaching her to love it.

Outside, the day resembled a Sherlock Holmes scene; thick fog enveloped the world and turned everything into a shadow of itself. Englemere Farm seemed like the creepiest place ever as they stood surrounded by fog and the ghosts of hundreds of Christmas trees with the sound of a chainsaw ringing in the distance. Not exactly romantic. Toula turned to say just that but noticed that she was suddenly alone.

"James?" She spun in all directions but couldn't see him anywhere. She tried calling his name louder, but there was no reply. She then realised there were no other customers in the field either. She was apparently out here alone. Who would go Christmas tree shopping on a farm on the foggiest day of the year?

Toula called his name again and heard the slight tremble in her voice which caused her to laugh at how ridiculous she was being. James was obviously hiding somewhere, waiting for the most opportune moment to scare her. Well, she would simply start looking for their tree, remaining super vigilant. She would show him that she wouldn't be frightened by him that easily. But somehow, James had crept back up to her and was standing so close that she smacked straight into him, making her jump and let out a scream. Toula hit him on the arm as he laughed and tried to hug her.

"You scared the life out of me," Toula shouted, more cross with herself than she was with James.

He wrapped his arms around her, kissing her hair as he apologised, which, she pointed out, trying to sound cross, meant nothing as he couldn't stop laughing while he said it.

"Come on, let's go find our tree," he said, taking her hand and trying to keep a straight face.

Choosing the perfect tree was going to be easy; Toula knew just what she wanted - four feet tall and fat. James hadn't given it even a second thought because a tree was a tree and so was happy to go along with whatever Toula decided.

After a while, however, what Toula decided was that she didn't like the idea of having a tree chopped down for them which would then die in a few weeks, so she chose a smaller, potted tree that they could keep forever and bring in every year.

They managed to get the tree onto the car roof, home, off the car roof, and into the corner of the living room without any problems. They stood admiring their first Christmas tree, still in their wellies and surrounded by dirt. "Right, I'll hoover this mess up, then grab the box of decorations from the loft so we can decorate," James said, wondering if they could get it done before the cricket match this afternoon.

"OK, I'll go get lunch started before *I* decorate the tree, and you watch the cricket."

James grabbed Toula around the waist and lifted her up.

"What did I do to deserve you?"

Toula laughed. "As tempting as it is to let you go on believing that I am completely perfect and utterly selfless, I just can't do it. The idea of someone, anyone, else helping me decorate the tree makes me twitchy, so as long as you help me with the lights, you are free from all other tree duties."

"Completely perfect!" James sighed, kissing her and putting her down.

That evening, once the tree had been dressed to

perfection and was twinkling in the corner, the cricket match had been a total success, and they had eaten James' 'famous' paella and *Nadiya Hussain's* actually famous, no need for air-quotes, mango and coconut cake, they curled up in each other's arms on the sofa and watched their favourite film, both trying to out-do the other by remembering the most lines.

Toula fell asleep replaying the weekend in her mind and wishing the days away until the next one. A few weeks ago, they had agreed to switch so that next weekend was also hers and she couldn't wait. How she had kept it a secret was completely beyond her.

Chapter 4

The sun sank lazily down into the bay through the pine trees, turning everything golden. The water was still, like a mirror reflecting the sky's beauty back at her. Sunrise and sunset were the best times of day to be outside, yet Toula and James always seemed to be in the car. Roll on the longer summer days when they would be able to go down to the beach after work for evening picnics and watch the sunsets without having to do so through the car window.

It was Friday afternoon, and Toula was driving, but not towards home.

"Come on, just tell me where we're going. Friday's car journey is always time for *The Weekend Game.*"
Toula focused more intently on the road ahead, feigning deafness.

"Can you pass me my Jammy Dodger, please?" she asked, all innocence. That morning, James had bought her a huge Jammy Dodger because it had a heart-shaped hole cut into it.

"I'm giving you my heart," he had said, all cheesy grin, pleased with himself.

"Nope, not until you tell me where we're going." James quickly put the biscuit in the door pocket where she couldn't reach it.

"Well, give it over because here we are, at our first stop."

James looked up and saw they were pulling into the train station car park.

Toula handed him an envelope which contained train tickets to London and a two-night reservation at a cute little boutique hotel in the heart of the city.

"What's all this?"

She could see that he was excited. "This is my turn to plan the weekend.".

James leaned over and kissed her. "You're incredible! I can't let you pay for all this, though."

Toula shut down the conversation right there. James never let her pay for anything, this weekend was her turn, and that was the end of it.

The hotel was stunning, quirky, and trendy with dark walls, sumptuous fabrics, and glossy wood.

They dumped their bags, had a quick shower, changed, and then headed out into the evening. It was a clear, crisp night; such a shame you could never see the stars in the city.

They didn't go far; it had been a long week, and they were in the mood to relax.

On the corner, they found a pizza place and wandered inside. The building had originally been a church, and the stained-glass windows had been cleverly lit to look as if the sun was streaming through them, overlooking the stripped wooden floor and tables, leather seating, and industrial lighting. A bar ran the length of one wall, and round cosy booths filled the far end.

James led Toula over to a booth and slid in, pulling her after him and wrapping his arm around her waist. He wasn't sure how he managed to keep his hands off her at work; he couldn't get enough of her. Luckily for him, Toula was a very tactile person too, and she enjoyed how he liked to be close to her. She ran her hand along his thigh under the table, looking up at him with a look that gave him the feeling they wouldn't be out late tonight.

They ordered a large seafood pizza and a bottle of wine to wash it down. While they ate, they chatted easily, vaguely watching the baseball game playing on the TV hanging behind the bar.

"So, we still haven't played *The Weekend Game*," James reminded her as he finished off the last of his wine. "What have you got in store for the next two days?"

"Well, I was thinking that maybe we should pop over to that Waitrose over the road and grab a bottle of whiskey and some profiteroles, go back to the hotel, snuggle up in bed and stick a film on, just take it easy because I have big plans for the rest of the weekend."

"I'm liking the sound of this already, although I do have a feeling that you're not actually going to play the game and just keep me guessing all weekend." James winked at her as he shot out of the booth to pay their bill before she had a chance to, knowing full well that whiskey and profiteroles meant that there was no way they would be getting to the film part of the evening.

They were up and out early on Saturday, starting the day in a coffee shop. As they sat in the window watching the world go by, the sky suddenly darkened, and huge splodges of rain began to fall.

James looked at Toula to try to make out her expression. She looked puzzled for a moment, then whipped out her phone.

"Plan A out the window? Is it back to bed for a day of food and sex?" He winked cheekily.

Toula laughed. "That was last weekend, remember? And last night! Do you really think I wouldn't have a Plan B?" She gathered up her things and put on her coat. "Let's go."

They spent the morning at Borough Market, letting their noses lead them around, eating all the freebies and testers they could find. The rain didn't last long, and by lunchtime, they were on their way to Covent Garden; this stop would've stayed on the itinerary regardless of the weather.

The lights were being switched on today, and Toula was so excited, but they still had a couple of hours, so they bought mulled cider and took their time wandering around the stalls and shops. Before long, the crowds started to grow, so they made their way over to get a good spot by the Christmas tree at the end of the market.

As the countdown began, James stood behind Toula, wrapping her in his arms and nestling his head against hers.

Three... Two... One. The lights burst into life, and the appreciative noises of the crowds grew around them. She felt him squeeze her tighter. Toula's eyes glistened as she stood looking at the tree, making the lights dance and blur together.

James turned her around so that they were facing each other, and he thought, once more, how beautiful she was. He saw how men looked at her, and he felt a weird mix of jealousy, pride, protectiveness, and love whenever it happened. He felt lucky that she had chosen him, and he didn't ever want to mess it up.

"Look up," he whispered.

Toula did, and a huge smile broke out across her face. He had positioned them perfectly underneath one of the giant mistletoe lights she had always wanted to come to see.

"Merry Christmas," he said, kissing her as if they were the only people in Covent Garden, London, the world.

That night, they went to a salsa club for cocktails and tapas; Toula even got James up dancing, which she knew he felt uncomfortable doing in front of other people and which made her fall in love with him a little bit more because he did it anyway, just to see the smile on her face. It was the early hours of the morning before they fell into bed, exhausted from the dancing, heady from the cocktails, happy with each other.

They slept late, checking out with just moments to spare. Leaving their bags with the clerk for the day, they headed out to find food.

"OK, today's schedule isn't fixed, so you have a choice of two activities, and lunch will be dictated by which activity you choose or, you can decide what you want to eat and have that determine the activity. We can have salt-beef bagels and play indoor crazy golf in Brick Lane, or we can have gyros and go ice skating."

Toula's plan went straight out the window because James couldn't decide what he wanted to eat. They wandered towards the tube station, and when he still hadn't chosen, she promised that whatever they didn't have today, she would make in the week, so he decided on crazy golf.

Brick Lane was heaving and they ended up eating their bagels standing on the street corner of the market, surrounded by lots of like-minded people who also didn't care that they were eating out in the cold because the bagels were *that* good.

And crazy golf was definitely well-named. They took their time in the Christmas-overhauled warehouse, full of passageways and odd-shaped rooms, each trying to let the other win; James because he knew Toula hated to lose and her because she knew that James knew this and wanted to be a better person for him. They both realised what they were doing quite early on and so agreed to simply play fairly, with the winner of each hole getting a kiss. Nobody could lose that way. They spent their time laughing and kissing. Toula won by one hole and managed to be a gracious winner, which was made easier by the discovery of a gyros van on the corner as they headed back to the station. It was a weekend that would have made the ideal Sunday-afternoon-straight-to-TV cheesy Christmas movie.

Chapter 5

They slipped out of the work Christmas party early, full of too much fizz and canapes, and jumped into the back of a taxi where they spent the journey giggling and kissing like love-sick teenagers. As they travelled along the beach road, James suddenly asked the driver to pull over.

"We'll walk from here."

The full moon hung fat and low over the ocean, and stars filled the sky, more than Toula had ever seen. She slipped out of her heels and squealed as her toes sank into the cool, damp sand.

James pulled her towards him, kissed her, twirled her around, and, right there on the beach, not caring how cold it was or if anyone was watching, just because they were caught up in the moment, they danced in the moonlight. Toula closed her eyes, relishing the feel of him pressed up against her, the sound of the waves the perfect musical accompaniment.

"Can I give you your Friday treat a little earlier this week?" he murmured into her hair. James' childlike eagerness for her Friday treats always made Toula feel so loved. She didn't open her eyes or say a word; she simply nodded. She felt him release her from his embrace and, when she opened her eyes, James was down on one knee in front of her. In his hand was a mini doughnut ring on a Christmas napkin which he had clearly swiped from the party buffet earlier. Toula laughed.

"One day," James said.

Toula knelt down with him and watched as he slipped the doughnut onto her finger.

"You know I'm gonna eat that, right?"

"OK but eat these first." He pulled out another napkin in which he had wrapped four tiny yum yums.

"Because you're yummy."

"*Mmmm*! You are the yummy one," Toula laughed, stuffing a doughnut in her mouth.

The next morning was a whirlwind of packing and trying to sneak Christmas gifts into their luggage. James had booked them a Christmas getaway, but that was all Toula knew, other than they were driving there, so that made the what-to-pack problem easier.

The long, sweeping driveway gave no clue as to what lay ahead. On one side was a thick pine forest which dappled the winter sunshine, and on the other, a deer park that led to more forest. The snow had begun to fall during the second half of their journey, and Toula hoped so much that it would settle so they could wake up to a white Christmas. As they rounded the final bend in the driveway, they were greeted by the most beautiful stately home Toula had ever seen.

James watched for her reaction as they pulled up to the house, and it made him burst with pride to see her face light up in surprise and delight. He reached over and squeezed her hand.

Around the entrance door hung extravagant fresh garlands, laced with Christmas lights and deep red velvet bows. This beautiful style followed through into the lobby where the lights from the decadent chandelier and decorations reflected off the marble floor. Toula felt as if she was being enveloped in a warm Christmas glow. New arrivals were treated to mulled wine in the main lounge while their coats and luggage were taken to their rooms.

James took Toula's hand and led her through the double doors. The lounge was breath-taking; plump, velvet sofas and deep tartan armchairs were set out to create separate seating areas, each lit by vintage standard lamps and tealights in ornate glass globes. At one end of the room, a roaring fireplace was crackling along as if trying to keep time with the crooning of Christmas songs.

In the corner next to the fireplace, and standing at least twelve feet tall, was the most beautifully decorated tree Toula had ever seen, topped with a shining gold star, and surrounded by golden presents, each finished with red velvet ribbon and bows.

They drank mulled wine and ate gingerbread stars, which had been hung on gold metal Christmas tree stands, and sat in the corner of the room, people-watching. Who would they be sharing their weekend with?

"So," James said after a while, "as much fun as the *Guess Their Life Story* game is, I think it's time to whisk you away and up to our room. This place has our whole weekend itinerary mapped out, but you're all mine for the next couple of hours, and I have plans of my own."

The room was incredible; warm grey walls, a Parisian style bed with rich, opulent coloured bedding piled high with plump cushions. A matching sofa stood in prime place, looking out of the enormous picture window at the garden, which had now been transformed into a winter wonderland by the snow and the fairy lights which adorned the trees. A Christmas tree decorated in gold and white stood in the corner of the room and, as she turned to admire it, Toula saw that James was putting a gift and an envelope underneath.

"No peeking or shaking or guessing," he laughed, walking through to the bathroom.

Toula searched through her suitcase until she found James' card and present and added them to his under the tree. He needn't have worried about her trying to work out what he had got her; Toula loved the anticipation too much for that. Their rule had been one gift not exceeding a set amount, which they had both exceeded.

James appeared back in the doorway wearing just a towel and holding a bottle of champagne,

"Shall we?"

Toula's bath at home was not big enough to fit them both in, but this one was enormous, copper, rolled-top with claw-shaped feet, now filled with beautifully-scented bubbles, surrounded with flickering candles, and plenty big enough for all the champagne-fuelled Christmas Eve fun they could think of.

"Toula, wake up!" James felt like an excited puppy, so eager for her to wake up and start their first Christmas together.

Last night, dinner had been followed by evening carol singing in the lounge where a piano stood next to the roaring fire. The snow had continued to fall outside, and as James had watched Toula singing along, his hand enveloping hers, he had wondered if he had ever been this happy. Now he was all impatience. He kissed her on the head, then all over her face, each time wishing her a Merry Christmas.

"Mmmmm, Merry Christmas, darling," Toula mumbled sleepily, pulling James on top of her and kissing him back, enjoying the weight of him on her. Suddenly, he leapt up and off the bed. He flung the duvet off her and pulled her out of bed.

"What are you doing?" Still half asleep, Toula let him pull her across the bed, loving that he was so excited but also wishing that he had made some... Ah! He *had* made coffee and had set it out on the table with an enormous bouquet of flowers.

"OK, sit here," James said, gesturing towards the sofa.

Toula curled up in the deep cushions and wrapped a throw around her shoulders. James swept the curtains open, bathing the room in the glorious light that only came when the world was blanketed in snow, and the sun was shining. Toula squealed and jumped out of the chair, almost sending the coffee pot flying. James scooped her up in a hug and swung her around.

"I was hoping so much that you'd get the white Christmas you'd been wishing for, and when I woke up to this, I couldn't wait for you to see it. Can I give you your present now?"

"OK, but let's have some coffee and enjoy this view for five minutes first."

"Always about the anticipation. OK, I concede." James poured the coffee and sunk into the sofa next to her.

The second Toula put her coffee cup down, James bounded over to the tree, bringing back a gift bag and a red envelope. They sat cross-legged at each end of the sofa, grinning at each other like fools. Inside the bag was a large, square, deep green box.

Toula looked up at him, taking her time opening it. James was practically giddy with excitement. Inside the box, nestled in white satin, was a silver chain with a thick mother-of-pearl disc pendant which had the sunrise etched into it in silver. Toula felt like her heart was going to explode. How had he known? She hadn't even mentioned it when she saw it on the antique stall in Covent Garden the previous weekend. She had suspected he would buy it for her there and then because she had paid for the London trip. More to the point, when did he buy it? They had been together the whole time. She looked up at him again, this time tears making her eyes sparkle. James had worried that Toula had seen him darting back from the antique stall to the coffee truck queue when she came out of the ladies', but the look of surprise on her face told him otherwise, so he explained.

"Now turn it over," he finished. On the back, the words, "For all our weekends" had been engraved, followed by a kiss.

Toula lunged across the sofa at James, throwing her whole body on top of him and covering him with kisses.

"I love it!" she squealed. "I love it so much. Thank you, would you put it on for me?" Once he had done so, she jumped up. "Your turn."

She ran over to the tree and brought back a perfectly wrapped box which sprinkled glitter in her wake. Excitement overcame him, and James had the thick brocade ribbon and the wrapping paper off in a second.

"You didn't?" he exclaimed, seeing what was in the box.

Toula had far exceeded their spending limit to buy him the watch he'd had his eye on for a while but wouldn't justify buying for himself. It was completely worth it just to see his reaction. She'd even measured his watch one night so that she could get the correct number of links taken out, ensuring it would fit him perfectly so he could wear it straight away.

James told her over and over that he loved it and that she was incredible and too good to him, and then a mischievous look settled on his face.

Toula looked at him, confused. "What's up?"

"Oh nothing, it's just that now I know you've broken the rule, it'll be a lot harder for you to tell me off for this." James handed her the red envelope. Inside was not a Christmas card, as she had imagined, but plane tickets to Greece and a brochure with a beautiful boat on the front.

"Two weeks sailing around the islands in July, all booked and paid for."

Oh, she could so tell him off for this! Compared to this, Toula had hardly even bent the rules, never mind broken them. Instead, she pushed all the gift boxes, ribbons, and bags aside, climbed onto his lap, took his face in her hands, and kissed him.

"Best Christmas ever," she smiled through their kisses.

"Best Christmas ever," he replied.

Breakfast was her favourite; smoked salmon and scrambled eggs on sourdough toast, washed down with Bucks Fizz.

Everyone arrived at the same time, as per the schedule, and wished each other a Merry Christmas, raising their glasses to one another across the room. The plan for the morning was to go on a horse-drawn carriage ride through the forest but, with the arrival of the snow, *Snowman Competition* and *Sledge Racing* had been added to the schedule, and they knew, just by looking at each other, that they would be doing that instead.

Six other couples had signed up to enter the snowman competition, and a trunk full of hats, scarves, carrots, and other snowman paraphernalia was brought out to the side lawn, which swept down to the now-frozen lake. They were given an hour to complete their perfect snowman, and everyone started off competitively, bustling about and raiding the trunk.

Interestingly, all of the snowmen were facing away from each other as if keeping their identities secret. All the couples finished early, and a snowball fight followed, started by an ill-timed throw at a spouse which accidentally hit the wrong person. The activities leader, who had returned from an archery lesson to judge the competition, found a screaming, laughing group, quite different from the serious, competitive one he had left.

Toula and James didn't win the snowman competition, and James declared in hushed tones, whispered into Toula's ear, that it was only because their snowman had been caught in the crossfire during the snowball fight and its head had fallen off.

They did, however, win the sledge racing. Toula beat each of the girls in turn, and James did the same with the men before they beat everyone in the couples' race. Hot chocolate was brought out and served before they all headed back to the house to get out of their wet, snow-caked clothes. Back in their room, they showered and put on the fluffy white robes, on which the hotel had had their names embroidered. Toula then dozed on the sofa with her head resting in James' lap while he sat reading.

The dining room had been transformed into a banquet hall with two rows of tables running down the centre to create a feeling of family. Although none of the couples had ever met before, they all got into the spirit of the day, pulling crackers, giving toasts, and chatting as if they were old friends. Couples were seated opposite each other and, even when they were talking to those around them, Toula could feel James' eyes on her. She wrapped her legs around his under the table. The food was incredible and thankfully, as it was so rich, there was a break between the main course and dessert when everyone was invited to go through to the lounge for the present giving.

James had wondered if there would be a guy dressed as Father Christmas, and they had joked about how awkward and cheesy that would be. Instead, the hotel manager gave the first gift, and each person chose the next gift for someone else until all the presents had been given out, and they then unwrapped them all together. Each couple received the same gift, a bottle of champagne, two champagne flutes, and a box of chocolates.

Dessert was followed by dancing and cocktails in the Orangery. Toula loved that James let go of his dancing inhibitions and spent the evening dancing with her. Maybe the salsa dancing in London had made him realise that he loved it too, or maybe it was just the whiskey sours.

The next morning, the sun streamed through a crack in the heavy-brocade curtains as if calling them to the day. They skipped breakfast, neither of them wanting to eat any more just yet, and headed outside, deciding against the horse-drawn carriage ride once more.

James took Toula's hand and led her for a walk along the forest trail. They talked about the previous day, both agreeing that the sledging was the bit they had enjoyed most, and about the past ten months. It certainly had been a whirlwind, and they had loved every second of it, especially their *weekend game* routine; each taking turns to decide the theme or activities kept things interesting and fun. Even though they didn't usually do anything extravagant, they were just happy in each other's company. They walked for hours and, by the time they got back to the house, lunch was being served and they were both ravenous.

Toula felt a tinge of sadness as she packed her things that afternoon. Sensing this, James stopped what he was doing and walked over to where she was standing, gathering her up in his arms.

"Thank you for an amazing weekend," he said, kissing her.

"Thank you," Toula replied. "You definitely won *The Weekend Game* this year."

"The year's not over yet," James reminded her. "New Year's weekend is your turn. I bet your plans blow mine out of the water."

Chapter 6

Because life's just like that, isn't it? Boy meets girl; they fall in love, everything is perfect. Blah, blah, blah. We've all read that story a million times.

Sorry to disappoint you, but this isn't that kind of story.

Remember right back in Chapter One when I told you that James and Toula were now in trouble? Remember even further back, on page one, I believe, when I first introduced you to James, I told you that he loves his family in the same sentence as I told you that he has dinner with his mum every Thursday? Very sneaky of me. I bet you were imagining him being the perfect son, taking shopping around for his mum, putting up shelves, mowing the lawn. Maybe you imagined he was also the perfect brother, protecting his sisters from suitors he felt weren't good enough for them, teaching them how to drive and, later, helping them to buy their first cars.

Well, yes, okay, he does all of those things, but that was not what I was talking about. The family I was referring to were James' two children, twin girls, Florence, and Amelia, who were just five years old.

"So what?" I hear you ask. Relationships break down; James is allowed to move on and have a new relationship. True. Except that he is still in that relationship. He lives at home with his wife and their two children. Now, before we start calling him names that I will not put into print, let me explain.

41

Three years ago, James and his wife separated but then she found out that she was terminally ill and James knew that she would rely on him for support and to be there for their children so he did what he believed was the right thing. He went back home.

And before we all start thinking badly of Toula for having a relationship with a man who is married to someone else, let me explain further.

Nothing you read in chapters two to five is true. Well, almost. James and Toula are crazy about each other. He buys the chocolates and the cakes, making up funny stories to explain why he chose them, and every Friday, they play The Weekend Game, taking turns to plan their perfect weekends. Then Toula and James say goodbye and spend the weekends separately. Never seeing each other outside of work. James talks about wanting to leave, but they both know it will never happen.

So now we find ourselves on New Year's Eve. Toula hasn't seen James since the last day of work before Christmas, almost two weeks previously, and has only heard from him once, as a reply to her Merry Christmas in the work group chat. That was until five minutes ago when he sent a message asking how she'd been.

James sent the message today because he was at home alone with the kids while his wife was at a hospital appointment with her mum. The message makes Toula feel like they're doing something wrong. While they flirt at work, there is no intention there and they have never acted on their feelings. The worst thing they do is play The Weekend Game and talk about their hypothetical life together, which, at first, was fun, but with the space to think that the last two weeks have given her, Toula has decided it needs to end. She just doesn't know how to do it. If they didn't work together, it would be simple. Now she stares at the phone, not knowing how to respond. Eventually, tired of re-reading his message and tired of thinking about it, she heads down the beach.

James had been irritable all morning; he couldn't settle on anything and found himself being short with the children, which he hates. He kept staring at the two blue ticks next to the message he sent Toula over three hours ago now, which meant that she had read the message but, for one reason or another, had chosen not to reply. Maybe she was angry with him for not being in touch before now, maybe she was out and had no signal or her phone battery has died, maybe she was trapped under her bookcase. In truth, he knew it wouldn't be any of those things, they had gotten to know each other inside and out, well, within the confines of a platonic relationship, and he knew that if she was angry, she would have let him have it. Both barrels.

He even knew what she was thinking, they were ten months into whatever this was, and they couldn't carry on like this indefinitely. He needs to think, and he can't do it here with all the noise of Christmas toys, all of which had required batteries to make them sing or make animal noises or shout instructions. He bundles the kids into the car, drops them at his mum's for an hour, and heads to the beach.

Wouldn't it be easy to have them spot each other along the beach, go running into each other's arms and declare their love for one another? A lovely fairytale ending. Unfortunately, as we said before, life's not always like

43

that...

James wandered along the beach, unaware of the sound of the ocean, of people walking their dogs, of the changing colours of the sky as the sun began its descent. James loved Toula with everything he was, he felt whole when he was with her and wanted all the things they had talked about. He knew that the longer this went on, the more chance he had of losing her. He was surprised that she hadn't been snapped up already and knew it was a matter of time before she met someone else, someone who could give her everything she deserved and who made her realise that waiting around for a maybe just wasn't good enough. He felt trapped, scared, and alone. His mind raced round and round in circles, not getting any closer to a conclusion. He needed to talk to Toula.

Fishing his phone out of his pocket, he dialled her number.

As Toula wandered along the beach, she noticed everything; families laughing, people throwing sticks into the waves for their dogs, every shade of pink, blue, purple, and orange that burst from the sky, the waves dancing over the pebbles sounding like bubble wrap, the tingling in her fingers because, even in her gloves, they were so cold, her heart beating under all the layers she was wearing, the thoughts swirling round and round in her head and crashing together.

Yes, she wanted to be with James, but she knew she needed to let go. His family needed him and that was far more important than whatever she was feeling. She bent down to pick up a heart-shaped pebble and tried to block everything out; the noises, the thoughts, the feelings, the families, the dogs, but it was taking an unhelpful amount of effort to do so. She grabbed a hot chocolate from the beach kiosk and headed towards the pier. It would be quiet under there at this time of day, with most people staying at the town end of the beach.

Just as she sat down, her phone started to ring, and she cursed herself for not putting it on silent.

James could hear Toula's phone ringing, not just down the line but close, out loud on the beach. As he turned the corner, he saw her get her phone out of her pocket and stare at the screen.

In the shadow of the pier, he couldn't make out her expression, but the fact that she wasn't answering made his heart sink.

Toula saw James standing there out of the corner of her eye and looked up.

He ended the call and put his phone away.

She took a deep breath and walked over to him.

There was no time to think for either of them. They both knew what they wanted and what they had to do about it. With an outpouring of emotions and with their words falling over themselves, all their plans for weekends together, of breakfasts in bed, trips to London and holidays on Greek Islands, forever after came crumbling down around them like a poorly constructed sandcastle. No more weekend games, no more dreaming, no more office flirtations.

It was time for her to move on and find someone new,

someone with whom she could have the kind of relationship she craved. It was time for him to focus solely on his family, to fill whatever time his wife had left with happy memories for their children.

And as both of their hearts broke, he kissed her for the first and last time.

And that is where we'll leave them.

Yes, work will be strange for a while, but they'll soon learn how to be around each other. They won't talk about what happened, and they will both be a little sadder.

After opening up to her friends back home about James, and being encouraged to move back to London, Toula will sell her beautiful house by the beach and buy a little garden flat in the city. She will accept a job at a large publishing company which she was previously head-hunted for but felt she couldn't stay for, needing to escape her heartbreak. She will move on, find love, and settle down. Her career in publishing will be a successful one. She will be happy.

James will lose his wife within the year and, devastated by both losses, he will switch himself off from love, devoting himself instead to his girls. While he knows that letting Toula walk away was the right thing to do he will often think of her and wonder, "What would we do this weekend?"

The End